women I don't know

and the lives I imagine for them

Jessica Matthews

E. E.

We pass each other
every day
carrying things no
one else can see.

She looks like her name is Beth.

Red polo. Khaki pants.

The kind of uniform that doesn't quite fit right.

She's buying oats.

Two boxes already in her basket.

I wonder if she eats them every morning.

Or if they sit in the cupboard next to three other

unopened packets.

She sits between them at a café table.

6

Strawberry milkshake too large for her hands.

Red-and-white straw bent slightly sideways.

She looks between the two women with her.

One older.

One somewhere in the middle.

Different faces.

The same eyes.

I wonder what parts of them she will grow into

without even realising.

She has three children with her.

None of them moving in the same rhythm.

One asking questions that never stop.

One trailing behind, distracted by everything.

One already at the exit before she is.

She doesn't raise her voice.

But there's a kind of fatigue in her shoulders

that feels older than the morning.

She keeps her hand near the youngest's back

without always touching them.

She's sitting in her car.

Engine running.

Windows up.

Her hands stay on the steering wheel

even though she's already parked.

Maybe she's waiting for someone.

Maybe she's waiting for a song to finish.

Or maybe she's just not in a hurry to go inside.

I think inside is where everything starts asking

things of her again.

She's waiting in line to order.

She seems a bit distracted,

a bit distant.

The barista has to ask her three times what she

wants.

She adjusts her sleeve a few times before

answering.

It isn't about the sleeve.

It's about the pause it gives her.

A small repetition that belongs only to her

before she has to make a decision.

She stands alone against the warm brick wall.

Sunlight across her face.

Eyes half-closed.

Her phone hangs loose in her hand.

Scroll.

Pause.

Tap.

I wonder if she saves things she means to come

back to…

and forgets,

not because she doesn't care,

but because there are already too many things

asking for her attention.

I see her most mornings.

Same time.

Same direction.

She walks quickly without looking rushed.

Like her body made a decision before the rest of

her caught up.

Sometimes she adjusts her bag strap twice in the

same block.

Sometimes not at all.

I wonder what happens on the mornings she

doesn't show up.

She stands in the freezer aisle longer than she
needs to.

Door open.

Cold air spilling around her legs.

Her shopping basket to the left.

Her hand hovers between two options and then

drops back to her side.

I wonder if indecision feels like relief sometimes.

She laughs before she finishes her sentence.

Her hand lifts slightly toward her mouth

then changes its mind.

The laugh comes out soft around the edges.

Gone almost immediately.

She looks at the person across from her

like she's checking whether it arrived correctly.

I wonder how many versions of herself she edits

before anyone else gets to meet them.

She chooses the longest checkout line.

Only three things in her basket.

She watches the conveyor move forward in small sections.

Someone sighs behind her.

She doesn't turn around.

I wonder if she came here because it was somewhere she was allowed to take her time.

She wipes down a table that is already clean.

The café is nearly empty now.

Chairs upside down on two of the tables.

Coffee machine hissing somewhere behind her.

She checks the clock above the counter

then keeps wiping in slow circles anyway.

I wonder if anyone is expecting her home.

Or if she's about to sit in her car for twenty

minutes before turning the key.

She waits at the pedestrian lights even though the
road is completely empty.

Everyone else crosses early.

She stays where she is.

Her coat looks too thin for the weather.

She keeps her arms folded tightly across herself.

The signal changes.

Still she waits half a second longer than necessary.

I wonder what other parts of her life she
approaches like that.

She bends down to tie her shoe.

Her hair falls forward across her face.

She leaves it there for a moment.

People move around her without slowing.

When she looks up, she catches me watching.

I look away first.

I wonder how many women are only fully alone

for three seconds at a time.

She laughs once into her phone,

a small sound

that doesn't fully leave her chest.

Then she stops.

Her face shifts slightly, like she is recalibrating

how much of herself is allowed to show.

I wonder who she becomes when she is alone

again.

She wears a pale blue cardigan with one button missing near the top.

Her hair is greying at the roots.

Not hidden.

Just there.

People move around her quickly.

She doesn't adjust her pace.

I wonder if she used to hurry more than she does now.

Or if something in her has decided there is no need to rush anymore.

She wears a dark jacket zipped all the way to her throat, even though it isn't particularly cold. Her hands stay inside her sleeves.

She looks like someone trying to keep herself contained.

I wonder if she feels safest when nothing is exposed.

Not even small things

She checks her phone,

locks it,

unlocks it again immediately.

Nothing has changed.

But she checks anyway.

The movement feels automatic now.

Like touching your tongue to a missing tooth.

I wonder when waiting for something became her

background setting.

She walks slightly ahead of everyone else.

Not enough to seem intentional.

Just far enough that nobody speaks to her without

speeding up first.

Her bag swings beside her,

slightly out of time with her steps.

I wonder if she knows she does it.

Or if her body has been leaving rooms before the

rest of her for years.

She stands at the roadworks holding the STOP

sign with both hands.

Traffic stretches behind her in patient little lines.

The fluorescent vest catches light harshly against

her skin.

When the sign flips to SLOW, the cars begin

moving immediately.

Nobody looks at her for very long.

She watches every windscreen as it passes

anyway.

I wonder how strange it must feel to control

movement all day.

She sits in a waiting room with perfect posture,

hands folded neatly in her lap.

Everything about her looks composed.

But her knee bounces slightly under the clipboard

where no one can see it.

I wonder when she learned to shake quietly.

She adjusts her hair in the reflection of a shop
window.

Quick movements.
Practised ones.

Then suddenly she pauses.
Looks at herself for a second too long.

Her hand drops immediately after, like she walked
in on herself doing something private.
The reflection stays there without her.

I wonder what she was trying to fix.
And whether it was ever about her hair at all.

She holds a takeaway coffee.

Cup warm between both hands,

lid untouched.

She stands still for a moment,

watching something pass in front of her.

Then she takes a small sip.

I wonder if she bought the coffee for the idea of

pausing,

and not for the drink itself.

She walks through the supermarket aisle.

Fluorescent lights flatten everything around her.

Her expression doesn't change.

But her eyes linger on things

longer than her hands ever do.

She reaches once, then pulls back.

Lets the item sit where it was.

I wonder what she is thinking about

instead of what she is buying.

She carries a canvas tote tucked high against her

shoulder.

It doesn't look heavy.

Still she adjusts the strap every few steps

like the weight keeps changing without warning.

I wonder how many women become strong in

ways nobody actually asks permission for.

She stands just outside the group.

Close enough to be included.

Far enough to not be noticed if she left.

She smiles at the right moments.

Nods along.

I wonder if anyone has realised

she hasn't said a single word.

She opens her car door,

then pauses before getting in.

Keys still in her hand.

One foot inside, one still on the footpath.

The door stays open longer than it needs to.

Like she forgot something.

Or remembered something she'd rather not.

I wonder how many moments in her day

feel like this -

almost moving,

then not.

She smooths the front of her shirt twice.

Then once more.

Her palms flatten the fabric carefully,

like she's trying to erase evidence of movement.

Her eyes drop briefly toward herself before lifting

again.

Quick.

Practised.

I wonder how many women learned to check

themselves before entering a room

the way other people check the weather.

She sits alone on a park bench.

People move past her in loose pieces.

Shoes.

Voices.

Shopping bags brushing against coats.

She watches them one by one like she's waiting

for someone to become familiar.

I wonder whether she's resting

or practising being nowhere for a little while.

She says my name three times during the phone

call.

Each time like she's placing it down carefully

between us.

There's a child crying faintly somewhere near her

end of the line.

She apologises for the noise before I even mention

it.

I wonder how many women are doing two lives at

once

with a headset pressed between them.

She laughs at something someone says.

It stays in the air a second longer than she seems

prepared for.

Something in her shoulders loosens slightly.

Almost imperceptibly.

I wonder how long it had been

since a sound left her body without supervision.

She picks up a box of cereal from the shelf.

Turns it over slowly.

Reads the side panel without changing expression.

Then places it back exactly where it was.

Edges aligned.

Facing forward.

Careful not to leave evidence she touched it at all.

I wonder what other parts of her life she returns

to order before walking away from them.

She walks beside her teenage son.

Bright voice,

exaggerated lightness,

trying to lift something invisible.

He shrugs her off in small, practiced ways.

Hands in pockets.
Feet dragging in the dirt.

She keeps trying anyway, like she hasn't decided

to stop yet.

I wonder if she is chasing the version of him that

used to meet her halfway.

She buys a skirt without trying it on.

The fabric rests folded over her arm,

still shaped by the hanger.

A mirror waits beside the change rooms.

She walks past without looking.

Still, her reflection appears briefly beside her

like something trying to keep up.

She doesn't slow down.

I wonder when she stopped needing to check

whether she existed correctly in other people's

eyes.

She stands at the entrance of the restaurant.

Warm light spills onto the pavement.

Glasses clink somewhere inside.

One hand rests lightly against the doorframe

while she looks in.

Only for a second.

People move around tables without noticing her

pause.

Then she turns and walks away.

I wonder what changed

in that small second.

She stands in the fast lane.

Water moving around her

like it expects her to begin.

Other swimmers pass in steady rhythms beside

her.

She stays near the wall.

One hand resting against the tiles.

Feet still planted on the floor beneath the water.

I wonder how many women spend their lives

accidentally standing in lanes built for people who

move faster than they do.

She stands at the edge of the playground.

Not sitting.

Not joining.

One foot slightly angled forward,

like she might step in at any moment.

Her eyes follow one child.

Back and forth.

Again.

I wonder if she measures distance

in seconds instead of steps.

She holds the lead loosely.

Wrapped once around her hand,

not pulled tight.

The dog stops often.

Sniffs everything.

Circles back,

then forward again.

She lets it.

Doesn't hurry it along.

I wonder if this is the only part of her day

that moves at someone else's pace.

She sits with a glass of wine and a cheese platter

meant for one.

The glass catches light when she lifts it

like something agreeing with her.

She cuts the cheese into careful little squares.

Not rushed.

Not performative.

Just paying attention.

I wonder how many women mistake survival for

living

until a moment this small reminds them there's a

difference.

She carries a helmet

but walks beside the bike.

One hand resting lightly on the handlebar.

The wheel turns slowly beside her.

Not riding.

Just guiding it forward.

I wonder if she planned to ride

or changed her mind along the way.

She stands at the self-checkout in a stretched

grey cardigan.

The machine beeps faster than her movements.

Unexpected item.

Please scan again.

A small frown settles between her eyebrows.

She rescans the same carton carefully

like the machine's disappointment might become

personal if she rushes.

I wonder how many women move through the

world apologising to objects.

She arrives early to the movie.

The doors aren't open yet.

Neat blouse.

Black trousers.

Practical shoes.

She stands near the wall watching people pass

without following any of them for long.

Her hands rest lightly on the strap of her bag.

Still. Patient.

I wonder if she has experience waiting for things

that begin late.

She is folding laundry in a laundromat.

Oversized jumper, soft at the sleeves.

The room is warm,

slightly humming with

machines.

She pauses between pieces,

staring at nothing in

particular.

I wonder if she likes this version of life that brings

her to a laundromat on Friday evenings.

She sits on the edge of a display bed in the

furniture store.

Dark jeans.

Hair clipped back loosely.

She doesn't lie down.

She presses her fingertips lightly into the

mattress, like she's checking whether softness

behaves the same everywhere.

Families move around her discussing colours and

delivery dates.

She stays very still.

I wonder how long it's been since she rested

somewhere that actually felt permanent.

She posts something vulnerable online

anonymously.

No profile picture.

No real name.

Just a paragraph written late enough at night

when honesty started sounding reasonable.

When people reply, she reads every comment

twice.

One of them says:

"God, I thought I was the only one."

She closes the app immediately after.

I wonder how many women are walking around

carrying entire secret lives that only exist in tiny

glowing rectangles after midnight.

She stands outside the shop studying the receipt.

Her purchases rest carefully beside her on the

pavement.

She folds the paper once.

Then again.

Her eyes drift somewhere past it before returning.

Cars move behind her in quick reflections of light.

I wonder if she keeps receipts

for the same reason some people keep old

messages.

Proof something happened exactly the way they

remember it.

She sits near the back of the bus in her school uniform.

Blazer folded beside her.

Shirt slightly untucked.

One earbud in.

The other hangs loose against her chest like she might still need to hear the world approaching.

Every few seconds she checks her reflection faintly in the darkened window.

Not fixing anything.

Just checking.

I wonder if she already knows how often being a girl means monitoring the version of yourself other people receive.

She walks through a bookstore,

seemingly lost in

her own thoughts.

Her glasses sit on top of her head,

headphones still in her ears.

No rush in her steps.

She touches spines without pulling anything out,

like she is browsing without permission.

I wonder if she still believes something might

recognise her first.

She unwraps the lollies carefully.

Hands steady, unhurried.

The paper comes away slowly,

folded back instead of torn.

A soft crease pressed into each layer.

She pauses between them.

Lets each piece fall open before moving on.

Nothing rushed.

Nothing wasted.

I wonder if she treats small moments

like they are the only ones that count.

She walks in the rain without changing pace.

Light jacket darkening at the shoulders.

Drops gathering along the seams.

Her hair clings softly to her cheek.

She doesn't brush it away.

Doesn't lift her hood.

Doesn't look for shelter.

I wonder if she has stopped negotiating with
weather
the way she has with everything else.

She stands outside the classroom talking to the
parents after school.

Fabric handbag at her feet.

Lanyard still around her neck.

She smiles through the conversation
automatically,

nodding at stories about lunchboxes and

forgotten hats.

Every few seconds her eyes drift briefly toward

the empty corridor behind her.

The building is getting quieter.

Still she stays.

I wonder how many women work entire days

inside other people's needs

then go home too emptied out to hear their own.

She sits at a table with others.

Voices rise and overlap around her.

She listens more than she speaks.

Her smile arrives slightly late,

then fades before the next person finishes.

She lifts her glass between conversations.

Small sips.

Something to hold.

I wonder if she feels most visible

in the pauses between other people.

She stands outside the playground fence holding

her phone up toward her children.

One is mid-laugh.

One already moving out of frame.

One blurred by motion entirely.

She waits a second longer before taking the photo.

Then another.

Like she's trying to catch the exact moment they

still belong partly to her.

I wonder how many mothers are quietly

documenting evidence

that somebody needed them this much once.

She pushes a trolley with only a few things in it.

The items sit loose in the basket,

rolling slightly at each turn.

The wheels click softly over the tiles.

She pauses at the end of each aisle without

reaching for anything immediately.

Then keeps moving.

Not hurried.

Not searching exactly either.

I wonder how many people come to supermarkets

for the comfort of existing somewhere brightly lit

among other lives.

She kneels in the dirt near the edge of the

playground.

A small bucket. A plastic spade. Hands already

brown with earth.

She presses the mud into shape carefully.

One pie. Then another. Then another.

No one joins her.

The other children move in loose clusters nearby,

calling out to each other, changing games without

announcing it.

She doesn't look up. She keeps making her pies.

I wonder at what age we learn to leave ourselves

behind in order to be included.

She stands holding two bunches of flowers.

One soft, pale, uncertain.

One brighter, more deliberate.

She turns them slowly in her hands.

Reads the small labels again, even though she

already knows what they say.

A tiny shift in her expression

before she puts one back.

I wonder if choosing has ever felt like revealing

something about herself she wasn't prepared to

see out loud.

She returns something to the counter.

No apology in her face.

Just certainty.

She places the item down carefully, as if it still

deserves respect even in refusal.

The shop assistant checks the receipt twice.

She waits without filling the silence.

I wonder how many women rehearse softness

when what they actually mean is no.

She struts down the street.

Light blue dress moving behind her,

soft and uncontained.

There's a lift in her step.

Her smile wide, reaching past her eyes.

She looks ahead like something has shifted in her

favour.

Her shoulders sit higher, lighter,

like they've forgotten their usual weight.

I wonder what just happened to her

that she hasn't told anyone yet.

She walks a few steps ahead of him.

Arms folded tight across her chest.

When she turns back,

her face sharpens,

words forming before they land.

But when she faces forward again, something in

her drops.

I wonder if she is more tired of being unheard or

of having to keep explaining herself.

She works at the pharmacy counter.

Her voice changes slightly with each customer.

Calm.

Efficient.

Warm where it needs to be.

She hands over the bag without rushing.

Next.

Next.

Next.

Between people, she rests her hands on the

counter

like she is waiting for something that belongs only

to her shift.

I wonder if she ever recognises herself

between one transaction and the next.

She starts her shift at 9pm.

The corridor already feels like 2am.

Bright light doesn't change anything about the hour.

She ties her hair up once.

Checks the board.

Moves.

Room to room.

Names she reads without slowing down.

I wonder if time behaves differently when your job refuses to acknowledge it.

She walks with a book open in her hands.

Eyes moving quickly across the page.

She adjusts her steps without looking up as people

pass her on both sides.

A small shift left.

A pause.

Then forward again.

Like the world is something happening just

outside the margins.

I wonder if this is the only place she feels fully

absorbed.

She walks the same loop almost every day.

Baby strapped close to her chest, small head

tucked in, fully surrendered to sleep.

Dog on the lead,

pulling slightly,

then circling back.

Her steps are steady, practised, like she's done

this a hundred times before.

She smiles as she passes, but doesn't slow down.

I wonder if this is the only way she gets the baby

to sleep

or the only way she gets out of the house without

being needed immediately.

She moves differently from the others on the

dance floor.

She twirls,

she shimmies,

she looks like the type of woman who sings loudly

in the car even at the red light.

I wonder if she comes every week,

or if tonight was simply the first night she let

herself feel free again.

She walks past me without noticing me.

Or maybe she does, and chooses not to show it.

Nothing in the moment changes.

No pause. No recognition.

Just two people continuing in opposite directions

with things we will never see in each other.

I don't turn around.

I let her disappear into the rest of the day.

I wonder how often I am the person someone else

almost remembers.

Thank you for spending time with
these quiet moments.

If you'd like to find more like this,
you can visit:

www.wildwomanpress.com.au

Jessica Matthews
Wild Woman Press